WHERE
OLIVER
FITS

The artwork in this book was created with puzzle pieces, glue, space unicorns and Photoshop.

The text was set in Palatino Sans Informal LT Pro.

Dedicated to everyone out there trying to find where they fit

Library of Congress Control Number: 2016956785

Text and illustrations
Copyright © 2017 by Cale Atkinson

Edited by Samantha Swenson
Designed by Colin Jaworski

Library and Archives Canada Cataloguing in Publication

Atkinson, Cale, author, illustrator
Where Oliver fits / Cale Atkinson.

Issued in print and electronic formats.
ISBN 978-1-101-91907-1 (hardback).—ISBN 978-1-101-91908-8 (epub)

I. Title.

PS8601.T547W44 2017   C813'.6   C2016-906923-0
                                              C2016-906924-9

Tundra Books, an imprint of Penguin Random House Canada Young Readers, a Penguin Random House Company

Published simultaneously in the United States of America by Tundra Books of Northern New York, an imprint of Penguin Random House Canada Young Readers, a Penguin Random House Company

penguinrandomhouse.ca

Printed and bound in China

tundra | Penguin Random House TUNDRA BOOKS

1 2 3 4 5 21 20 19 18 17

WHERE OLIVER FITS

Cale Atkinson

tundra

Do you ever wonder where you fit?
Could it be here?

Or maybe over here?

Oliver wondered too.

Oliver couldn't wait
to see where he fit!

He wanted to be part of something exciting...

Something wild...

Something out of this world!

On his first try...

It didn't go so well.

His second try wasn't much better.

And on his third try...
Well, all he got was a laugh.

"Being myself is getting me nowhere," Oliver thought.

"Maybe I have to be more like them and less like me."

"If they want red, I can be red."

It worked, at first.
The red pieces were happy to see Oliver.

That is,
until
the
red
rubbed
them
the
wrong
way.

Then Oliver thought,
"Okay, forget my color, how about my shape?
If they want square, I can be the squarest there is."

Oliver tried lots of things.

Too tall.

Too short.

Too pointy.

Too bulky.

Not right.

All wrong.

But no matter what Oliver
did or how hard he tried,
all he heard was

no!

No!

NO!

"That's it!" Oliver shouted.
"If someone else is what they want,
someone else is what they'll get!"

In a flurry, Oliver cut, taped and glued until …

He was nowhere to be seen.

"I'll be sure to fit THIS time."

"Oh, hello there!" the other pieces greeted him.
"Please join us, friend. We love your fancy shape,
and what fetching colors!"

"Where were you hiding? Where have you been?"

Oliver joined them,
and guess what?

He fit!

He fit so well that no one
had a clue it was really him.

Everything was perfect.

Except ... everything didn't *feel* perfect.

In fact, it didn't feel right at all.
"If I have to hide and pretend I'm someone else,
am I really still me?" Oliver thought.

"And if I can't be me, then what fun is it to fit in?"

So he took off his disguise.
"You!" they shouted.
"Boo!" they shouted.

Oliver was glad to be himself again,
but he was also back to being alone.

"I don't fit anywhere," he thought.
"How can I be part of something exciting,
wild or out of this world if it's just me?"

But when Oliver looked up,
what did he see?

He wasn't alone!
Others had taped, cut and glued in
search of their fit too.

Oliver discovered that you can't
rush or force your fit.

All you can do is be yourself!

Your fit will find you.
And it will feel …

Don't forget, no puzzle is complete
without every last piece,
including you—and Oliver too.